MY OFFICIAL FUN-TASTIC BARBIE ANNUAL 2002

Name: Caitlin Mair

Age: 6 six

Starsign: ee brin

Favourite colour: brew

Best friend: Claire and Emma

I love Barbie because: She is cool.

When I grow up I want to: singur

Written by Jane Clempner
Designed by Sheryl Bone
Cover designed by Julie Clough

Published in Great Britain in 2001 by
Egmont World, an imprint of Egmont Children's Books Limited,
239 Kensington High Street, London, W8 6SA
Printed in Italy. ISBN 0 7498 5322 0

CONTENTS

FUNHOUSE

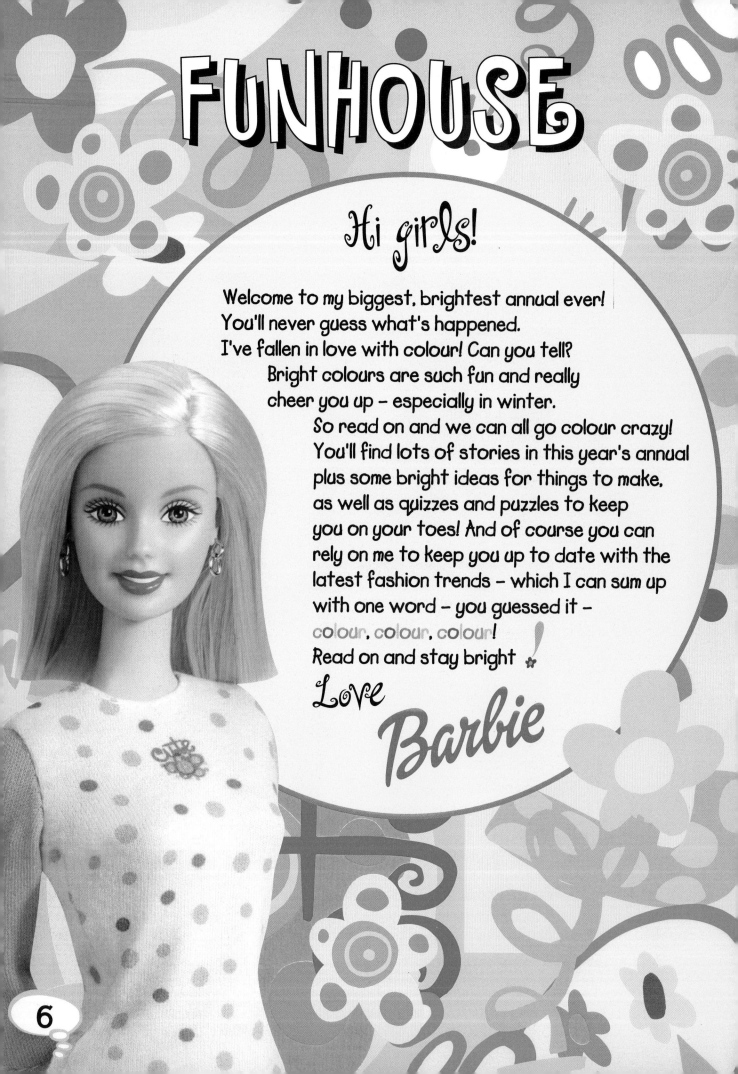

Hi girls!

Welcome to my biggest, brightest annual ever!
You'll never guess what's happened.
I've fallen in love with colour! Can you tell?
Bright colours are such fun and really
cheer you up – especially in winter.
So read on and we can all go colour crazy!
You'll find lots of stories in this year's annual
plus some bright ideas for things to make,
as well as quizzes and puzzles to keep
you on your toes! And of course you can
rely on me to keep you up to date with the
latest fashion trends – which I can sum up
with one word – you guessed it –
colour, colour, colour!
Read on and stay bright

Love

Barbie

Winter is Fun-Tastic!

Take a tip from me and put a spring in your step this winter! Get out and have some fun!

Smile

Here are 10 reasons I just lOVE Winter

Building snowmen

Ice-skating

Wrapping presents for friends

Hot chocolate

Woolly hats and long scarves

Real fires

Snowball fights

Christmas trees

Dreaming of summer

Skiing

All the fun of the fair!

"Look at the blue sea!" said Barbie.

"And our lovely suntans!" sighed Teresa.

It was a wintry afternoon and Barbie, Kira and Teresa were sitting by the fire, looking through their holiday snaps.

"Can I keep this one?", asked Kira. "I lost my camera so I don't have any photos of my own."

"Of course. Cheer up!" said Barbie. "Perhaps you'll get a camera for Christmas!"

"Yes," said Teresa, "stop being so gloomy! Winter isn't all bad. There's fun to be had somewhere. We just have to find it!" Barbie leapt up in excitement. "I know just the place!" Minutes later, the friends were on their way! It was a short drive to the coast and soon the bright lights of Pleasure Beach were in view.

"Brrrrr!" said Kira, getting out of the car and pulling on her woolly hat. "It's too cold to be outside!"

"Come on," said Barbie. "Let's warm up in here!"

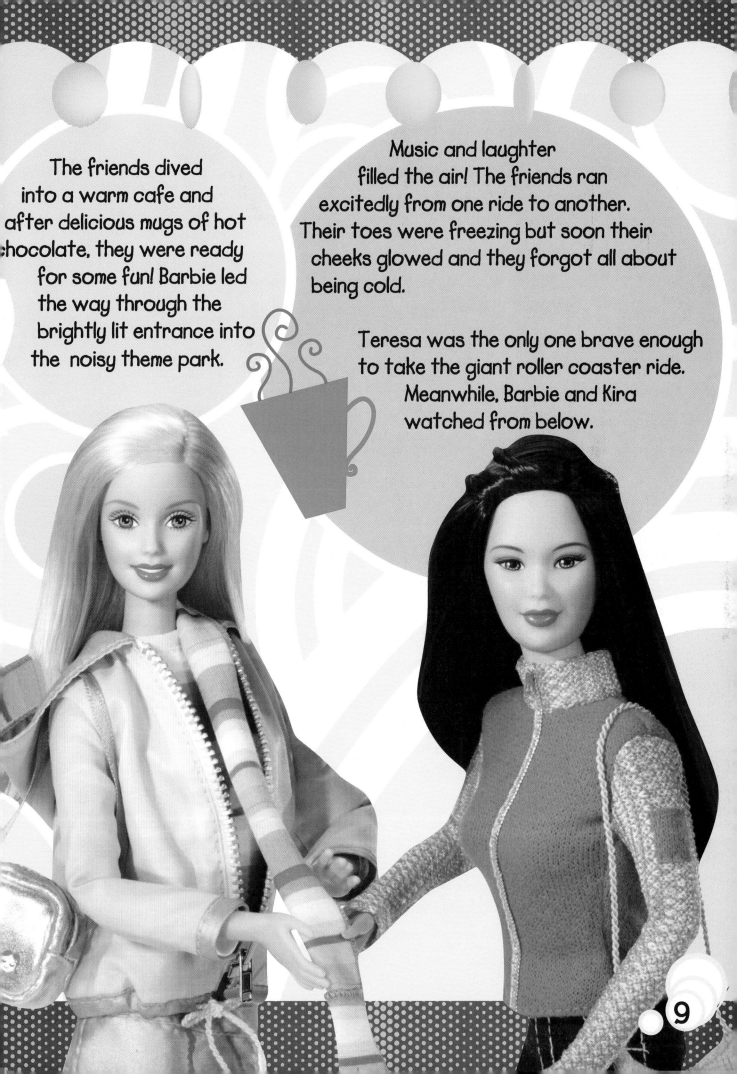

The friends dived into a warm cafe and after delicious mugs of hot chocolate, they were ready for some fun! Barbie led the way through the brightly lit entrance into the noisy theme park.

Music and laughter filled the air! The friends ran excitedly from one ride to another. Their toes were freezing but soon their cheeks glowed and they forgot all about being cold.

Teresa was the only one brave enough to take the giant roller coaster ride. Meanwhile, Barbie and Kira watched from below.

"What's that?" said Barbie, gazing towards a small, dark tent. The words above the entrance beckoned to her with twinkling fairy lights: 'Madame Zena Mystic Readings Only £5.00'. "Ooh, gosh, I can have my fortune told!" said Barbie.

"Five pounds! You must be joking! It's all nonsense!" laughed Kira.

"I know," said Barbie, "but I'll take a chance!"

She slipped between the heavy curtains and waited for her eyes to get used to the darkness. A strange woman appeared from the shadows and lifted the cloth from her crystal ball. "Do not be nervous," she said in a funny foreign accent. "Ze crystal ball only sees ze happy future." Barbie handed over her money. "I see a vonderful future ahead for you, my dear. You will have ze good fortune. Yes... I zee it clearly... good fortune very soon. You are a good person, my dear, with a good heart and you vill do a good deed that vill make many persons happy. And finally... oh yes... you vill fall in love!"

Barbie blinked as she stepped back out into the lights and noise of the funfair. Her friends were waiting for her.

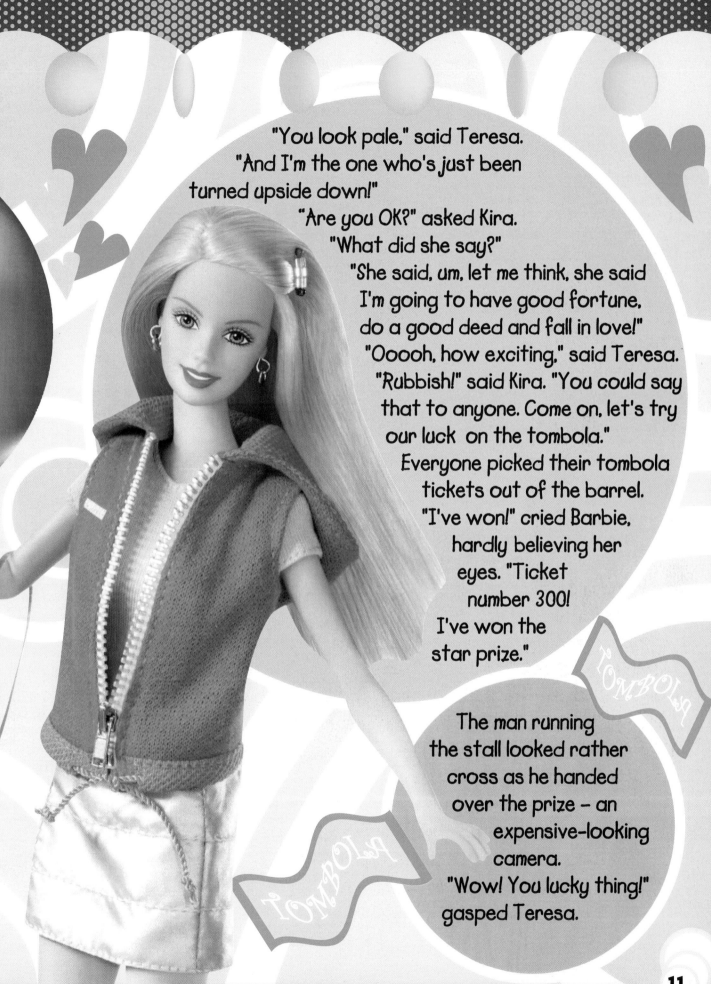

"You look pale," said Teresa. "And I'm the one who's just been turned upside down!"

"Are you OK?" asked Kira. "What did she say?"

"She said, um, let me think, she said I'm going to have good fortune, do a good deed and fall in love!"

"Ooooh, how exciting," said Teresa.

"Rubbish!" said Kira. "You could say that to anyone. Come on, let's try our luck on the tombola."

Everyone picked their tombola tickets out of the barrel.

"I've won!" cried Barbie, hardly believing her eyes. "Ticket number 300! I've won the star prize."

The man running the stall looked rather cross as he handed over the prize – an expensive-looking camera.

"Wow! You lucky thing!" gasped Teresa.

"It's my good fortune... just like the fortune-teller said!" smiled Barbie. Then she had an idea. She turned to Kira. "I already have a camera, so I'd like you to have this one – to replace the one you lost."

"Oh no, I couldn't."
"You can... and you must! There. That's my good deed too! You see all Madame Zena's words are coming true!"
"You know what that means, don't you," said Teresa, excitedly. "Next you are going to fall in love!"
Barbie blushed.

The friends left the hustle and bustle of the funfair and linked arms as they walked back towards their car. In the dark street, only the late night shops were still open. The music from the funfair faded away and soon the sound of their footsteps echoed in the dark street.
"What was that?" said Barbie, bringing everyone to a sudden stop.
"What? I can't hear anything," said Teresa.
"Shhsh! A noise. Coming from over there, from those dustbins."
"Be careful," warned Kira, as Barbie crept towards the noise.

"It sounds like... " Barbie
lifted the lid. "Aah... oh look!"
There, huddled into a pile of old boxes,
meowing sadly, was a little grey kitten.
Barbie carefully lifted the frightened
creature from its uncomfortable bed.
"Oi! What are you up to?" A rough-looking man
had come running from the shop and was waving
his arms at them. "Get away from my bins and
take that scruffy animal with you!"
Barbie gazed at the kitten and wrapped it lovingly
inside her coat. "That's it!" she said. "I've fallen in love!"
As she stroked its soft little head the kitten began to
purr. "And guess what I'm going to call her –
Madame Zena!"
She was one fortune-teller they
would never forget!

PURR PURR PURR

FUNHOUSE

Aries

March 21 – April 20

Lucky Colour: Red
Look good in: Big, chunky sweaters
What's ahead: You will make a new friend and learn the truth about someone.
Remember: The more you give, the more you receive!

Gemini

May 22 – June 21

Lucky Colour: Yellow
Look good in: Hats, scarves and gloves
What's ahead: You will take up a new sport or hobby and meet a whole new crowd of friends. Life will be full of excitement!
Remember: Be confident – you will go far!

Taurus

April 21 – May 21

Lucky Colour: Blue
Look good in: Anything denim
What's ahead: You will realise how important your friends are and you will face some new challenges – and succeed!
Remember: Don't bottle things up – let your feelings show!

Cancer

June 22 – July 22

Lucky Colour: White
Look good in: A funky new image!
What's ahead: You might worry too much about pleasing others – try to work out what YOU want – and stick to it!
Remember: Chill out!

Leo

July 23 – August 23

Lucky Colour: Gold
Look good in: Jingly jewellery
What's ahead: You will be the leader of the pack and friends will ask your advice.
Remember: Share your wisdom!

Virgo

August 24 – September 22

Lucky Colour: Silver
Look good in: Something shiny
What's ahead: There are exciting times ahead and you will have to make some important choices.
Remember: Try something new!

FORTUNES

Libra

September 23 – October 22

Lucky Colour: Pink
Look good in: Something sporty
What's ahead: Yours is the luckiest sign of the zodiac and you will be more popular than ever.
Remember: Share your good fortune!

Scorpio

October 23 – November 21

Lucky Colour: Black
Look good in: Something soft and furry
What's ahead: Decisions need to be made. Trust your own feelings and listen to your closest friend.
Remember: Believe in yourself!

Sagittarius

November 22 – December 21

Lucky Colour: Purple
Look good in: A new jacket or coat
What's ahead: You will discover who is your true best friend and you will meet a special new friend.
Remember: Have more fun!

Capricorn

December 22 – January 20

Lucky Colour: Orange
Look good in: Anything bright!
What's ahead: You will be wise and calm and take everything in your stride.
Remember: Don't change!

Aquarius

January 21 – February 19

Lucky Colour: Pale Blue
Look good in: Something with a hood
What's ahead: You will put problems behind you and share happier times with your friends and family.
Remember: Never settle for second best!

Pisces

February 20 – March 20

Lucky Colour: Green
Look good in: Something long and floaty
What's ahead: You will be creative and energetic and discover new skills.
Remember: Be yourself!

Fun Zone

Know Your True Colours

Did you know that the colours you choose reveal your true personality?
Look in your wardrobe. Which colour do you wear most?
Read on and discover your inner secrets!

Red

You are a bit of a drama queen! Red is the colour of love and danger! You like to be noticed and have lots of confidence!

Yellow

Bright and cheerful, this is the colour of summer. You are warm hearted and want to spread happiness to others.

Pink

Pink can be baby soft or funky and fluorescent. You love fashion and follow trends and have bags of personality.

Black

Sophisticated and mysterious, black is the colour that commands respect. But do you wear it to protect yourself and hide your true feelings?

Green

This is the colour of independence. You never follow the crowd but like to do things in your own special way.

Blue

The coolest of colours, blue shows that you have a strong head and a soft heart! You are romantic and have lots of secret dreams!

16

Over the Rainbow!

The seven colours of the rainbow are
hidden in this word search. Can you find them all?

```
Y T U I F L R O R R E D Z R T
E R L M R N A R S S G E I N D
L E L J O D T A K L P D N G E
L H S G R E E N F W P I D S B
O R T Y P S V G B L U E I X Z
W V I O L E T E J K I S G P F
B A R Y I R S D D U O L O V E
```

RED   ORANGE   YELLOW   GREEN
BLUE   INDIGO   VIOLET

Answer on page 60.

17

Simply Superb Activity Zone

Match the pairs

Kira has been practising with her new camera –
she's hoping to be a fashion photographer.
Of course Barbie was happy to pose!
Can you match the shots into 3 identical pairs
and find the odd one out?

Find the letters

Find the letters that only appear once to make a phrase that every photographer knows!

T	S	F	R	M	N	X
O	B	I	T	L	B.	D
F	X	N	D	O	R	E

Barbie is lost.

Can you show her the way back to her friends?

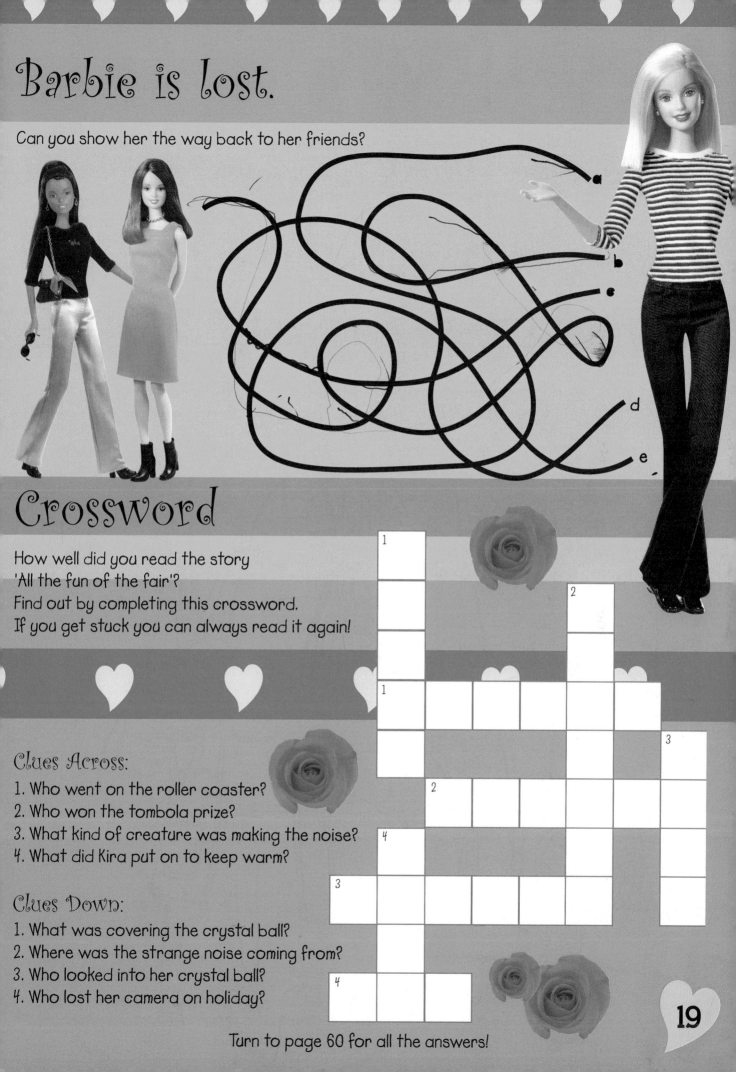

Crossword

How well did you read the story
'All the fun of the fair'?
Find out by completing this crossword.
If you get stuck you can always read it again!

Clues Across:
1. Who went on the roller coaster?
2. Who won the tombola prize?
3. What kind of creature was making the noise?
4. What did Kira put on to keep warm?

Clues Down:
1. What was covering the crystal ball?
2. Where was the strange noise coming from?
3. Who looked into her crystal ball?
4. Who lost her camera on holiday?

Turn to page 60 for all the answers!

19

Colouring Crazy!

I love taking photographs – just like Kira!
Colour this picture of me using your favourite colours!

This is a picture of me on holiday last year in Hawaii.
The flowers were very colourful and my grass skirt was
yellow – colour me in to see what it was like.

21

I've taken my latest, dazzling collection of designs to the most glamorous locations in the world!

I always send a postcard home. Can you work out which well-known cities I have visited?

Barbie xxx

TO: All my friends

ADDRESS:

Back home

in England

Pussy cat, pussy cat,

where have you been?

I've been to

LONDON

Answer on page 60.

I N L M A N L M A

nscramble these letters to find a fashionable city.

M i l a n

Sent with love...

...from

P a r i s

Change one letter of this flower to find this ancient capital.

R o m e

Greetings

...from the city that never sleeps!

N e w   Y o r k

... Love From Barbie xxx

All wrapped up!

This is the season for parties!
I love parties – any excuse to dress up and have fun!
One of the best things about a party is wrapping
the present! Here's how to make your presents really
special (the only problem is, they might look too good
to open!):

It's easy - and lots of fun - when you know how!

1 Lay the present, face
down, on the paper to see how
much you need. Use scissors to
cut the paper neatly.

2 Make sure the present is in
the middle of the paper before folding
in the edges. The paper should be
tight before you stick it down.

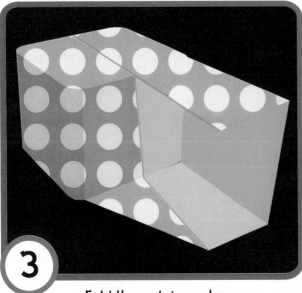

3 Fold the ends in as shown.

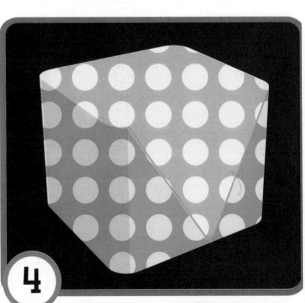

4 Now, turn your package over.
It is ready to decorate!

There are lots of ways to make your present look special:

1

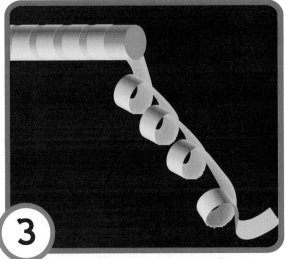

Make your own wrapping paper by decorating plain paper with potato prints, stencils or glitter. (You could trace over the border on this page to make a heart-shaped stencil).

2

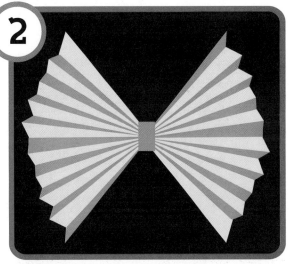

Make a butterfly bow by folding coloured paper over and over in a concertina. Then pinch the middle together and hold with sticky tape or a little piece of ribbon.

3

Use different coloured gift ribbons and create lots of beautiful curly bows.

4

Use real ribbon to make a simple bow. Try to co-ordinate your colour scheme.

5

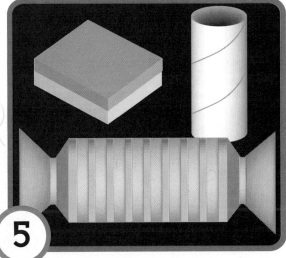

Disguise a funny-shaped present by putting it in a gift box or bag. Or use a tube and make it look like a cracker!

6

Make your own gift-tags from card and ribbon or by cutting shapes from last year's Christmas cards.

25

SECRET AGENT BARBIE

When I see my ideas come to life on the catwalk it is an amazing feeling! But this season it almost didn't happen at all! Let me tell you the story...

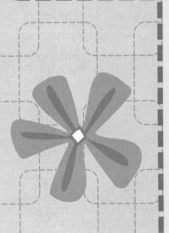

I was working late, putting the final touches to the designs for my new collection, when my mobile rang: "Hi Barbie, it's Misha. Remember me?" "Misha?" I gasped. "Gosh, I haven't seen you since college! How are you? Are you still doing that top secret job?" "Yes... that's why I'm calling... I need... Barbie, you're the only... " And the phone went dead!

I felt all tingly and cold. Why was she ringing me so late at night? Her voice had sounded strange. I hardly slept at all. I felt I had to do something. So, the next day I searched through my old address book and found the name of the government office where Misha worked. I put on my most business-like outfit and went straight over.

26

"I'm sorry," said the stern-looking receptionist, "if you don't have a security pass, you can't come in."

Head of Department

I waited until she was busy on the phone, slipped by, ran up the stairs and pushed open the door marked 'Head of Department'.
The woman sitting behind her desk was speechless.
"I'm a friend of Misha," I said, not giving her time to argue, "I know she's in trouble and I won't leave until you tell me why."
The woman looked me up and down, and then composed herself and smiled.
"My dear, there's no need for you to worry," she said. "Misha has been working too hard lately and I have given her time off and... and she's gone skiing."
I didn't need to hear any more. I turned and left.

Now I knew for sure that something was wrong. Misha had broken her leg in a skiing accident when she was little and vowed never to go near the slopes again!

I sat down on a park bench to consider what to do next when my phone bleeped. It was a text message:

HELP! COME ALONE
WHERE? 2ND HOME
WHEN? MUM ON PHONE

Now I was scared. A coded message! I looked around the park nervously. Was I being watched?

I went straight home. I knew exactly what the message meant. Misha was asking me to meet her at our favourite café – we used to call it our 'second home'.

I knew I had to go alone, and I had to be there on *Sunday* at 6pm – the time that Misha's mother used to phone her every week for a chat. It was a good thing that we had been such close friends!

I arrived fifteen minutes early and waited. It was winter and as dark as night outside. My coffee went cold. I seemed to wait forever, but then the café door opened and Misha appeared, disguised in a heavy coat and dark glasses. She sat down at the table and grabbed both my hands. She was cold, and shaking.

"Th... thank you for coming. You're my last hope."

"Wh... what's going on?" I stuttered. "Are you OK?"

"Just listen. We're both in danger. Serious danger. I've been working undercover. There's a group of bad people who are stealing collections from top designers, copying them and selling them on the black market under their own label. And YOU, Barbie are their next target!"

I was speechless. Misha continued.

"But I've blown my cover. They're on to me. I've... I've been threatened. I have to stay in hiding. So you are my only hope, Barbie. You're the only one that can stop them... Will you do it?" I nodded. She continued.

"Then here's the plan... "

The next morning I put the designs for my new collection into my briefcase and took a taxi to the airport. I acted as if everything was normal.

As the taxi pulled out into the busy street I looked behind. It was just as I expected. I was being followed!

It was Monday rush hour and the streets were busy. I put on my dark glasses and clutched my precious briefcase tightly. The taxi driver decided to try a short cut. We swerved into a narrow alleyway. The car behind followed. We drove quickly down the narrow passage when, suddenly, the brakes screeched! It was a dead-end! I pushed the door and jumped out just as the other car arrived, blinding me with its headlights. I was trapped! A figure ran towards me and pulled my case from my hands. There was nothing I could do.

As the villains sped away with my briefcase, I sighed a huge sigh of relief. Everything was going to plan!
"Well done!" said Misha, getting out of the driver's seat of our 'fake' taxi.
"Good driving!" I joked.
"I wouldn't want to do it again," she sighed. "Now, let me check my watch and see if the remote control tracking device in your briefcase is working. If it is, we can trace them all the way back to their headquarters!"

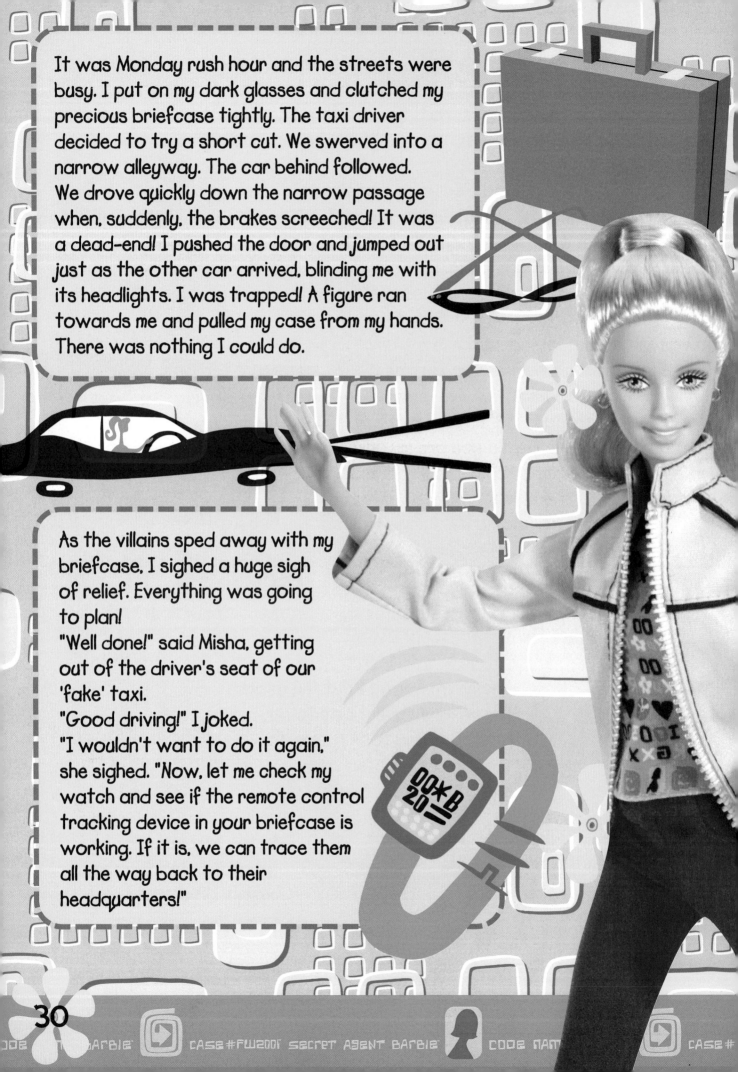

Misha pressed a secret button on her watch and picked up the bleeping signal loud and clear. "Hop back in and we'll follow *them* this time!" she said.

The signal led us back into the centre of the city.

"I thought they would be hiding out in some remote place," said Misha, "not right here under our noses!"

"Look!" I said. "The signal has stopped..." I looked up. "Here!"

"That can't be right!" said Misha. "This is where I work!" We ran up the steps into the building that I had visited so innocently a few days before. Misha showed her pass and the receptionist let us through. The signal led us up the stairs... and into the room marked 'Head of Department.' Misha burst in and I followed. There was the woman I had spoken to – Misha's boss, just about to force open my briefcase and steal my designs!!

"It was YOU all along!" said Misha. "It's no good trying to run for it. The police are right behind us. You're going to prison, where you belong!"

Head of Department

Two weeks later, we were sitting at our old table in our favourite café.

"I've been made the new Head of Department!" beamed Misha.

"You deserve it!" I smiled. "You were so brave!"

"You too, Barbie. Here, I have something for you."

She handed me a card. It said: Secret Agent Barbie. "You are now an official secret agent and I will call on you whenever I need help!"

I smiled. "That's what friends are for," I said.

SECRET AGENT I.D. CARD

CODE NAME : BARBIE™

NAME :

SECRET CODE :

33

Secret Agent

Being a Secret Agent is lots of fun.
I love sending coded messages to my friends!   Here's how it's done!

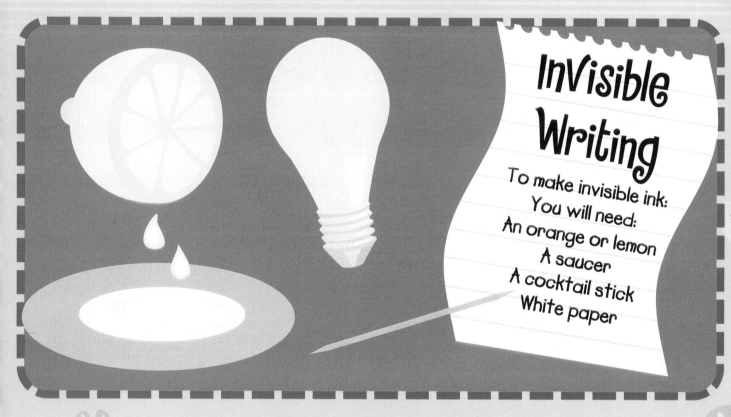

Invisible Writing
To make invisible ink:
You will need:
An orange or lemon
A saucer
A cocktail stick
White paper

1. Squeeze the juice of the orange or lemon into the saucer.
2. Dip one end of the cocktail stick into the juice.
3. Write your message on the paper.
4. Hold the paper over a warm radiator or light bulb and the writing will appear!

BARBIE™ BARBIE™ BARBIE™ BARBIE™ BARBIE

Writing in Code

Each letter of the alphabet is replaced by a number – but don't start at number 1 – that's too easy! For example:

A=22 B=23 C=24 D=25 E=26 F=27 G=28 H=29 I=30 J=31 K=32 L=33 M=34 N=35
O=36 P=37 Q=38 R=39 S=40 T=41 U=42 V=43 W=44 X=45 Y=46 Z=47

Fun Zone

Watch your secret messages and pictures appear as if by magic!

InVisible Writing # 2!

You will need:
white paper
a white candle
poster paints
and paintbrush

PAINT

Simply write your secret message on the paper using the candle.
Then, when you are ready to reveal the secret, paint over the paper
and your message will appear!

BARBIE™ BARBIE™ BARBIE™ BARBI

Can you read this message?

34 26 26 41   22 41   40 30 45

23 39 30 35 28   41 29 26   34 36 35 26 46

Answer on page 61

Puzzle Zone

Here's a message written in code!
Can you crack the code and read the message?

ENKKNV SGNRD ENNSOQHMSR

Answers on page 61

Can you find 10 flowers in the picture below?

 Answers on page 61

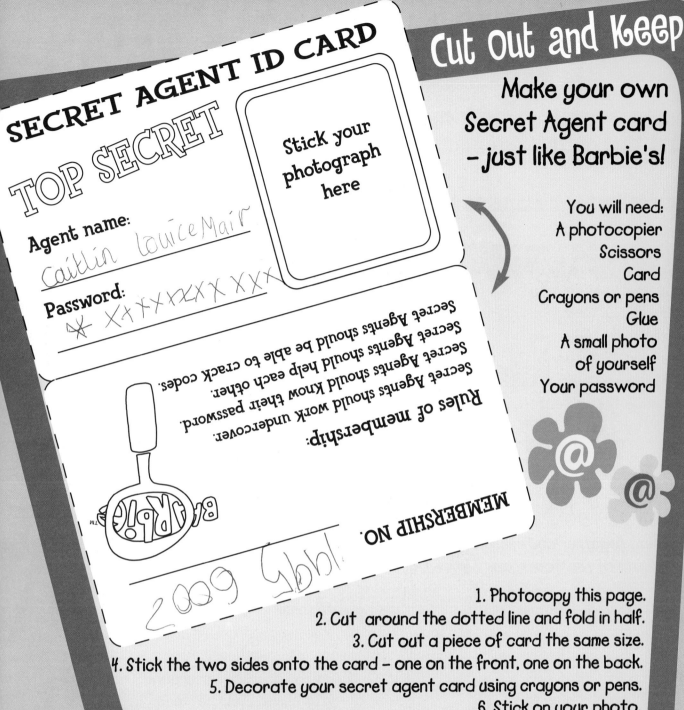

SECRET AGENT ID CARD

TOP SECRET

Agent name:
Caitlin LouiceMair

Password:
✗ ✗ ✗ ✗ ✗ ✗ ✗ ✗

Stick your photograph here

Rules of membership:

Secret Agents should work undercover.
Secret Agents should know their password.
Secret Agents should help each other.
Secret Agents should be able to crack codes.

MEMBERSHIP NO.

2009 9661

Make your own Secret Agent card – just like Barbie's!

You will need:
A photocopier
Scissors
Card
Crayons or pens
Glue
A small photo of yourself
Your password

@ @

1. Photocopy this page.
2. Cut around the dotted line and fold in half.
3. Cut out a piece of card the same size.
4. Stick the two sides onto the card – one on the front, one on the back.
5. Decorate your secret agent card using crayons or pens.
6. Stick on your photo.
7. Write in your name and password – in code, of course!

Now you can start your own Secret Agent Club and ask your friends to join!

SECRET AGENT ID CARD

TOP SECRET

Agent name:
Secret Agent Barbie

Password:
✱✱✱✱✱✱✱

37

FRIENDSHIP QUIZ

Do you have one special friend? Or lots of friends?
What kind of friend are you?

Answer these questions to find out...

1. Your friend has a new hair style.
You're not impressed. When she asks
what you think, do you:

a) Tell her its a disaster
b) Tell her it looks fab
c) Tell her she always looks nice
d) Change the subject

2. At school you overhear some girls
saying nasty things about your best
friend. Do you:

a) Join in the conversation
b) Rush to tell your friend everything
you've heard
d) Walk up to the girls and tell them
not to gossip
c) Forget it – they aren't worth it

3. There are a group of girls at school
who play together and seem to be
having lots of fun. Would you:

a) Feel miserable because you
are left out
b) Stick with your best friend
– she's all you need
c) Ask if you can play too
d) Walk straight over and join in!

4. You find your best friend
in tears and she won't
say why. Do you:

a) Tell a teacher
b) Get so upset that you start
crying too
c) Comfort her and keep everyone
else away until she feels better
d) Demand that she tells you what's
wrong so that you can help.

NOW CHECK YOUR SCORES:

Mostly a's
Do you sometimes feel left out?
It really isn't difficult to make friends.
Just try being a little more tactful
and think of other people's feelings.
Otherwise you could end up
being very lonely.

Mostly b's
You make a wonderful 'best friend'.
You probably have someone that you're so close
to that people call you 'The Twins'. You go
everywhere together and think the same thoughts!
But remember – variety is the spice of life! There
are lots of other interesting people out there too!

5. Your Mum says you can have a friend to stay for the night. Do you:

a) Say no thanks. You don't like sleepovers
b) Invite the one friend that you always ask
c) Ask if you can invite two people as it would be more fun
d) Find it too hard to decide who to choose

6. You and your best friend have been given the same top for Christmas. Do you:

a) Tell your friend to take hers back
b) Make plans to wear them at the same time
c) Have a giggle when you turn up looking the same
d) Take yours back – you don't want to look sad

7. Your friend has given you a new Barbie doll outfit for your birthday. But it's one you already have! Do you:

a) Ask for the receipt so you can take it back
b) Hide the old one away and put the new one straight on Barbie
c) Chill out – Barbie can never have enough clothes!
d) Put it to one side and give it to someone else for their birthday

8. Your best friend has been playing with someone else more than with you. Do you:

a) Forget about her – she wasn't much of a friend anyway
b) Ask her if you've done something wrong?
c) Wait for her to come back to you – she is your best friend after all
d) Find someone else to play with

Mostly c's

You are the best kind of friend there is! You know how to respect other people's feelings and how to be kind and caring. All your friends are important to you but there is someone who is special to you. This is the friend you will probably keep all your life!

Mostly d's

You are the life and soul of any party! Always popular and easy to get along with. Lots of people count you as their friend. But don't be afraid of opening up and getting close to people – one day you might need one really special friend to rely on.

So Special!

Barbie and her friends were in their favourite café discussing an important matter:
"It's Christie's birthday next week," Kira was saying, in a hushed voice.
"What shall we do? She's the girl that has everything!"

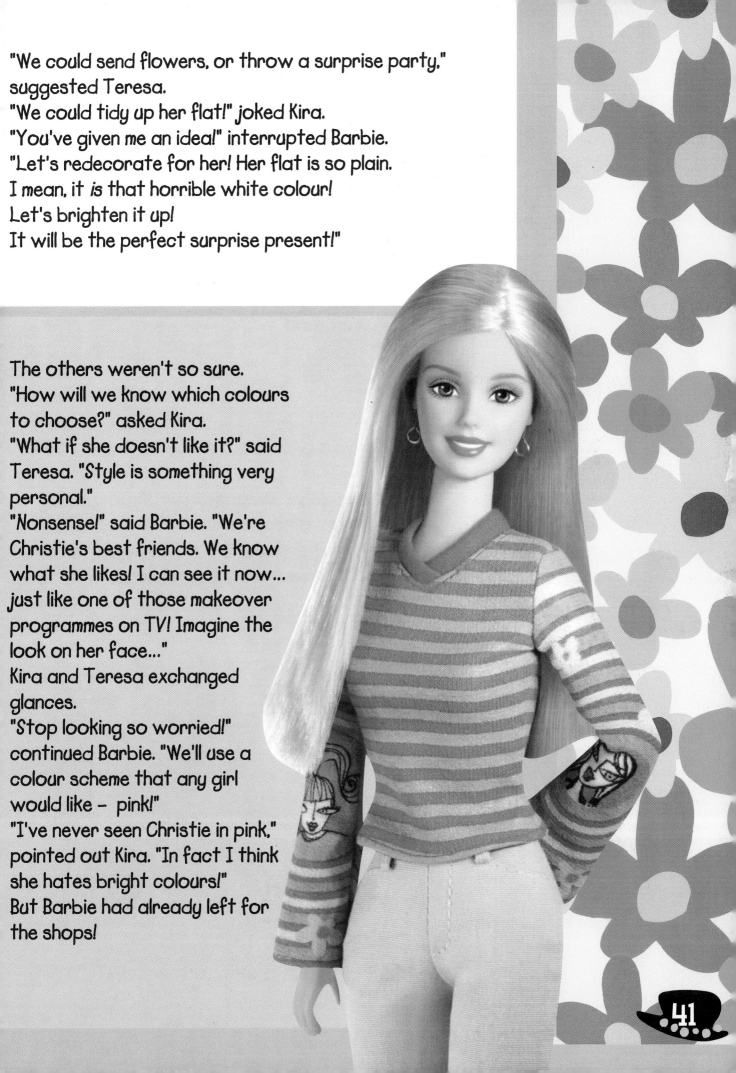

"We could send flowers, or throw a surprise party," suggested Teresa.
"We could tidy up her flat!" joked Kira.
"You've given me an idea!" interrupted Barbie.
"Let's redecorate for her! Her flat is so plain. I mean, it *is* that horrible white colour! Let's brighten it up!
It will be the perfect surprise present!"

The others weren't so sure.
"How will we know which colours to choose?" asked Kira.
"What if she doesn't like it?" said Teresa. "Style is something very personal."
"Nonsense!" said Barbie. "We're Christie's best friends. We know what she likes! I can see it now... just like one of those makeover programmes on TV! Imagine the look on her face..."
Kira and Teresa exchanged glances.
"Stop looking so worried!" continued Barbie. "We'll use a colour scheme that any girl would like – pink!"
"I've never seen Christie in pink," pointed out Kira. "In fact I think she hates bright colours!"
But Barbie had already left for the shops!

"What do you think?" asked Barbie, spreading out a large piece of paper on the floor of her bedroom. "I've designed Christie's flat to make it look like the inside of her favourite designer clothes store! She'll love it! The bedroom becomes a dressing room and the living room has shelves and a seating area. Well?"
Kira and Teresa were silent.

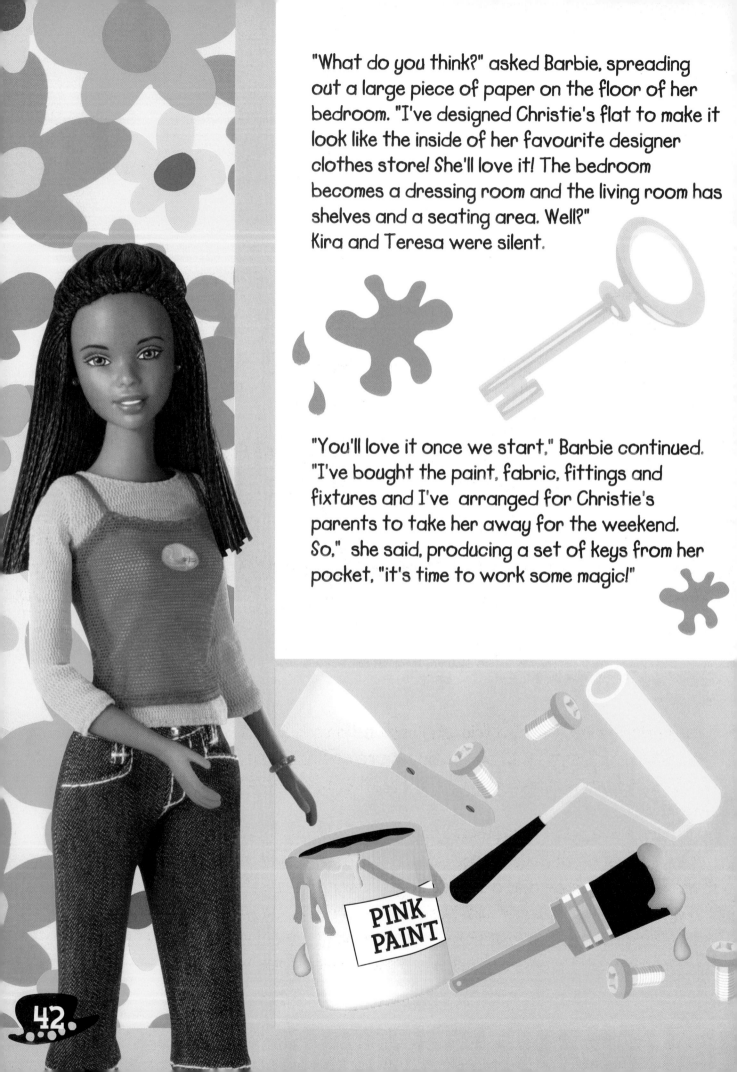

"You'll love it once we start," Barbie continued. "I've bought the paint, fabric, fittings and fixtures and I've arranged for Christie's parents to take her away for the weekend. So," she said, producing a set of keys from her pocket, "it's time to work some magic!"

PINK PAINT

Rather reluctantly, Barbie's friends followed as she led the way into Christie's flat. They set to work and as the day wore on Barbie's enthusiasm began to rub off and they worked so hard that by the following day the transformation was complete.

They stood back to take a look. Everything was ready. There were flowers and magazines on the table, clothes and accessories on the shelves; curtains at the bedroom door and a sign saying: Dressing Room. It was an exact copy of a certain funky designer clothes store – Christie was in for a surprise!

"Wow!" said Barbie. "It's even better than I imagined. She is *so* going to love this. I can't wait to see her face when she arrives home tonight."

They didn't have to wait long. They held their breath as the door opened and Christie turned on the light.

"Surprise!" they shouted, jumping out from their hiding places. Christie immediately dropped her suitcase and clasped her hands to her face. "I ... wh ... what ... where am I?" she stuttered.

"Do you like it?" said Barbie, rushing over to her and taking her by the arm. "Come and look at everything. It's for your birthday. A surprise. Now you can wake up every day in your favourite shop!"

Christie stood still and looked around. Slowly it began to sink in. The colour came back to her cheeks and her expression of shock changed – to one of horror!

"What have you done!" she asked, staring at her three friends. "My flat... my home. It's awful!"

Barbie, Kira and Teresa were stunned into silence.

"It's... it's so... pink!" she continued. "Who's idea was this?!"

Barbie stepped forward. "Don't blame the others," she said, bowing her head in shame. "It's all my fault. I talked them into it."

Christie tried to smile. "I'm sure you meant well. But you should have asked me first!"

"I see that now," said Barbie. "Just because I like bright pink it doesn't mean you do too!"

"Even the best of friends can have different tastes," agreed Christie. "Anyway, there are still two days before my birthday – anyone want to help me decorate?"

By the day of her birthday Christie's flat was transformed once more – back into her favourite colour – white! She was so pleased that she decided to invite everyone round for a combined birthday and flat-warming party.

"I'm sorry I'm late," said Barbie, arriving last. "I've been shopping! I wanted to get you something special."

And she handed Christie a small gift. Everyone watched as Christie unwrapped it.

"A bright pink mobile phone!" she laughed. "I love it, Barbie. It's perfect. Every time I use it I will think of you!"

"And next time I decide to surprise you I'll phone and ask you first!" joked Barbie.

And it turned out to be the best birthday ever.

Colouring Zone

Barbie is getting ready for a big night out.

Choose your favourite colours to bring the pictures to life.

47

Your Bedroom Makeover

Here are some tips and ideas on how to brighten up your bedroom in no time at all!

Use mirror-tiles to make your bedroom look bigger!

Add colour with a bright throw on your bed and lots of cushions

PINK PAINT

Paint the walls – paint the furniture if Mum will let yo

Hang a notice board with your favourite photos, pictures and cards

Rearrange your furniture

Make a stencil to create your own border

Buy or make some free-hanging shelves and fill them with all your favourite things

Decide on a theme or colour scheme and stick to it!

My Special things™

Barbie is so excited! Kira, Christie and Teresa have all arrived for a sleepover!

"I love your pretty pyjamas, Barbie!" says Kira, joining the others in the living room.

"And your slippers are so cute!" replies Barbie.

"I've brought some new nail varnishes," says Christie.

"I've baked cookies," smiles Kira.

"And the pizzas are ordered!" giggles Barbie. "All we need now," she says, pressing the remote, "is a really good video!"

The music starts and the girls settle on the settee.

"Anyone brought tissues?" asks Teresa. "I always cry – even if it's not sad!"

"Me too," says Barbie. "I cry most when there's a happy ending!"

"What are we watching?" asks Christie.

Just then, the titles appear on the screen.

"Cinderella?!" they all say at once.

"Yes," laughs Barbie. "I couldn't resist it in the video store. It's set in the modern world so it should be fun!"

The girls settle down and watch, pausing only when the pizzas arrive.

"I like this version of Cinderella," says Teresa, munching on her slice of ham and pepperoni. "It seems so true to life!"

"Me too," says Kira. "The handsome Prince is soooo gorgeous!"

They enjoy the video so much that, even though they know the ending, they all cry when the slipper fits!

"That was so lovely!" says Christie, wiping her eyes.
"Do you think anything like that ever really happens?"
"Of course!" says Barbie. "True love always finds a way!"
"Talking of 'true love'," grins Teresa,
"have you seen much of Ken lately?"
"Well, actually," says Barbie, in a way that
makes everyone listen, "he has invited me to
a big party at his parents' house in the
country – next weekend!"
"Wow!" breathes Kira.
"What will you wear?" asks Teresa.
"Can I come?" jokes Christie.
The girls chatter and gossip, forgetting
all about the time. Christie has brought
some new nail varnishes and they
have fun painting each
other's nails.

Kira has brought some cucumber and
cornflower facemasks. She tries it on Barbie
but Barbie giggles so much that the facemask won't set!
"Don't go to the party like that!" jokes Kira. "You look
a nightmare!"
"Let me put your hair up for you," says Teresa.
"And I'll do you some really fab make-up!" says Christie.
"Barbie – you *shall* go to the ball!"

Half an hour later Barbie is allowed
to look in the mirror.
"It... it's certainly different!" she says
"It's a bit over-the-top" admits Christie.
"It's not you at all! You looked better before!"
Barbie washes off the make-up and lets down her
hair. "How about cookies and milk!" she says, trying to
take her mind off the party.
The girls chatter and giggle until Barbie
looks at the clock and realises it
is midnight!

"I guess we had better think about
sleeping!" she says, stifling a yawn.
So, they spread the bedroom floor with
mattresses, duvets and pillows.
They dim the lights and
try to sleep.
Barbie opens her diary.
"Next weekend," she
whispers to Kira who is
lying next to her. "It's so close!
I have to look my best. What do you think
I should wear? Should I change my hair?
Wear it up? Try something new?"
"Stop panicking!" says Kira. "You don't have to
look different – just be yourself. Ken's friends
will love you as much as he does!"
"Thanks, Kira. I know I'm being silly."
"That's better. Now get
some beauty sleep!"

But no matter how she tries,
Barbie can't sleep. She listens to the
sound of her friends' breathing.
She can hear the bedroom clock ticking.
The moonlight is shining through the curtain
and reflecting in the mirror.
Barbie tosses and turns.

Then suddenly the alarm is ringing and it's time to
wake up! Barbie looks around but all her friends have left
already – she must have overslept. How strange, they didn't
say goodbye. She looks at the calendar.
"Oh gosh!" she says, "It's Saturday! The day of the party!"
She looks at her watch.
"What's happening?! It's time to leave!" And when she looks around, there
on the bed is the most beautiful ball gown she has ever seen! The dress
fits her perfectly and, before she has time to think, she is walking in to
the party! Everyone turns and stares. Kira, Christie and Teresa –
what are they doing here? They are still wearing their pyjamas!
Why are they laughing? Barbie suddenly realises they are laughing
at her. She rushes to look in the mirror. Oh no! She has forgotten
to wipe off the facemask and she's left her curlers in her hair...
"Argh!!!" Barbie wakes up with a scream.
"Wh... what's the matter?" says Kira.
"It was... a nightmare!" sighs Barbie. "My worst nightmare!
Thank goodness it wasn't real. I was at the party and...
oh it's too horrible to think about!"
"Go back to sleep," says Kira. "That's what
you get for eating cookies at bedtime!"

And the next weekend Barbie walks into the most 'grown-up' party of her life. But this time she isn't wearing a big floaty ball gown and fancy make-up. She is just being herself. And guess what? She looks like a real princess.

In Your Dreams?

What will you be when you grow up? Someone famous?
What kind of job would suit you best? Find out in this fun quiz.

1. Which of these would be your perfect pet?

a. A hamster in a colourful cage of mazes
and runs

b. A white Angora rabbit

c. A Golden Labrador to take for long walks

d. A collection of rare insects

**2. Which word best describes
your school bag?**

a. Wacky

b. Glitzy

c. Sporty

d. Heavy

**3. Which kind of party would you most
like to be invited to?**

a. Fancy Dress

b. Sleepover

c. Ice-skating or roller blading

d. A party with games and competitions

**4. Which subject do you enjoy
most at school?**

a. Art

b. Drama

c. P.E.

d. Maths

**5. You have a day off school.
Do you:**

a. Re-vamp your bedroom

b. Paint your nails and do your hair

c. Go swimming

d. Catch up on your homework

6. Which are you happiest wearing?

a. A T-shirt and jeans you
decorated yourself

b. Your dressing-up clothes

c. Your tracksuit

d. Your school uniform

**7. What would be your ideal Christmas
present?**

a. An art set with pens,
pastels and paints

b. A tiara

c. A new bike

d. A microscope or telescope

**9. Time to snuggle up with a
good book. Would it be:**

a. An action adventure

b. A Barbie magazine

c. You're too busy to read

d. A mystery story

What your score means:

Mostly a's:

Wow! You are bursting with creative energy and talent! You have a wonderful imagination and can always be relied on to come up with fresh ideas. If you develop your skills you could become a famous artist or designer, or perhaps a writer, illustrator or photographer. Go for it!

Mostly b's:

A princess in the making! You are a real 'girly' girl and love all the most luxurious things in life! As there aren't many Handsome Princes to go round, perhaps you should make your mind up to work your way to the top, run your own business and employ others to do the work for you!

Mostly c's:

Wait for us! You never sit still for long! You love fresh air and are always on the go. You don't like to be tied down and would hate a desk job. If you work and train hard you could reach the top as a world-class athlete, an explorer or conservationist in the Amazon! With your energy and enthusiasm, anything is possible!

Mostly d's:

You are one to watch! With your thirst for knowledge you thrive on study and investigation. You love to get to the bottom of things and put your considerable brainpower to use. You have a great future – possibly as an inventor, scientist or doctor. Could your work one day change the World?

A Mixture:

Confused? NO! Multi-talented! Just take your pick. You have so many skills to choose from! It's up to you. Put your mind to it and work hard and YOU can achieve anything. In fact you could be the next Prime Minister!

Dreamtime Puzzles

Which outfit matches this slipper?

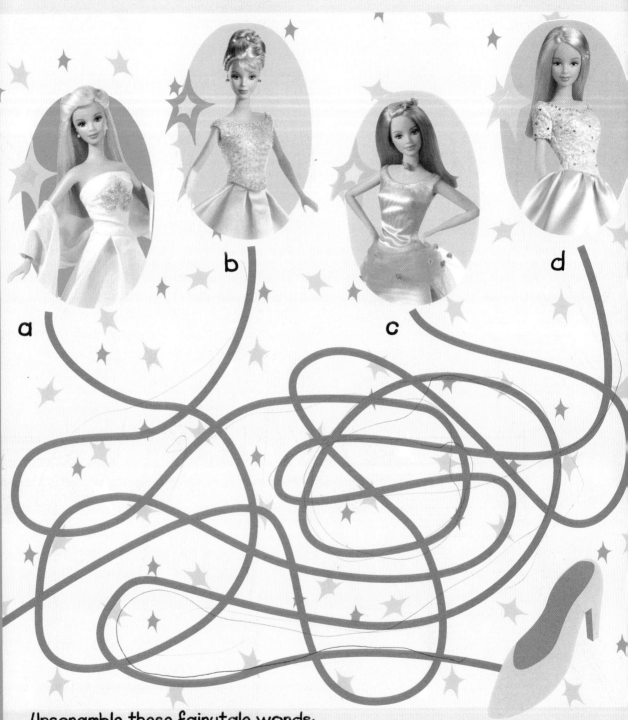

a

b

c

d

Unscramble these fairytale words:

cepsinsr	epnirc	lgbalwno
princess	*prince*	
psilpre	lpsel	phayp dinneg

58

Turn to page 61 for answers

A Fairytale Ending!

Use your crayons and pens to make Barbie look like a real princess!

All The Answers!

Over the Rainbow – Page 17:

Y	T	U	I	F	L	R	O	R	R	E	D	Z	R	T
E	R	L	M	R	N	A	R	S	S	G	E	I	N	D
L	E	L	J	O	D	T	A	K	L	P	D	N	G	E
L	H	S	G	R	E	E	N	F	W	P	I	D	S	B
O	R	T	Y	P	S	V	G	B	L	U	E	I	X	Z
W	V	I	O	L	E	T	E	J	K	I	S	G	P	F
B	A	R	Y	I	R	S	D	D	U	O	L	O	V	E

Matching Pairs – Page 18: 1+6, 3+5, 4+7.
Number 2 is the odd one out!

Find the letters – Page 18:

T	S	F	R	M	N	X
O	B	I	T	L	B	D
F	X	N	D	O	R	E

SMILE!

Barbie is lost – Page 19: Answer: b

Crossword – Page 19:

...Luv from Barbie – Page 22:

London

Paris

Change one letter of this flower to find this ancient capital!
Rome

Greetings ... from the city that never sleeps!
New York

Unscramble these letters to find a fashionable city.
Milan

Writing in code – Page 35:

Answer: MEET AT SIX BRING THE MONEY

PUZZLE ZONE – Page 36:

Answer: FOLLOW THOSE FOOTPRINTS
Each letter has been replaced by
the one BEFORE it in the alphabet!

Dreamtime Puzzles – Page 58:
Outfit b matches the slipper.

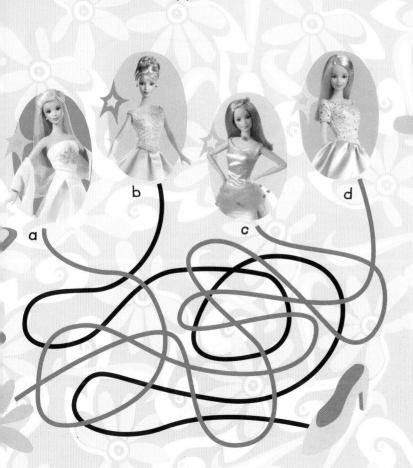

a

b

c

d

Unscramble these
fairytale words:

cepsinsr	–	princess
epnirc	–	prince
lgbalwno	–	ball gown
psilpre	–	slipper
lpsel	–	spell
phayp dinneg –		happy ending